"Makes you think thoroughly before
making a decision."
—Hassan Stevenson, age 11

"I have read five different stories in
one night and that's a record for me.
The different endings are fun."
Timmy Sullivan, age 9

"It's great fun! I like the idea of
making my own decisions."
—Anthony Ziccardi, age 11

AND TEACHERS
LIKE THIS SERIES, TOO!

"We have read and reread,
wore thin, loved, loaned, bought for others,
and donated to school libraries, the
Choose Your Own Adventure® books."

CHOOSE YOUR OWN ADVENTURE®—
AND MAKE READING MORE FUN!

Bantam Books in the Choose Your Own Adventure® Series
Ask your bookseller for the books you have missed

Choose Your Own Adventure® Books for younger readers

YOUR CODE NAME IS JONAH

EDWARD PACKARD

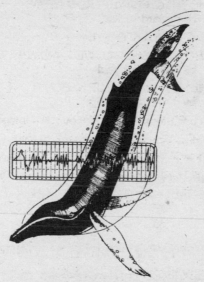

ILLUSTRATED BY PAUL GRANGER

BANTAM BOOKS
TORONTO · NEW YORK · LONDON · SYDNEY

RL 5, IL age 10 and up

YOUR CODE NAME IS JONAH

A Bantam Book / January 1980

2nd printing .... February 1980	6th printing .... March 1981
3rd printing .... April 1980	7th printing .... July 1981
4th printing .... July 1980	8th printing ... December 1981
5th printing ... September 1980	9th printing .... March 1982
10th printing ..... August 1982	

Original conception of Edward Packard

CHOOSE YOUR OWN ADVENTURE® is a
trademark of Bantam Books, Inc.

Artist: Paul Granger

ISBN 0-553-23182-0

Published simultaneously in the United States and Canada

Bantam Books are published by Bantam Books, Inc. Its trademark, consisting of the words "Bantam Books" and the por-
trayal of a rooster, is Registered in U.S. Patent and Trademark
Office and in other countries. Marca Registrada. Bantam
Books, Inc., 666 Fifth Avenue, New York, New York 10103.

PRINTED IN THE UNITED STATES OF AMERICA

O   19 18 17 16 15 14 13 12 11 10

YOUR CODE
NAME IS JONAH

WARNING!!!!

Do not read this book straight through from beginning to end! These pages contain many different adventures you can have while working as a secret agent. From time to time as you read along, you will be asked to make a choice. Your choice may lead to success or disaster!

The adventures you take are a result of your choice. *You* are responsible because *you* choose. After you make your choice follow the instructions to see what happens to you next.

Remember—you cannot go back! Think carefully before you make a move! One mistake can be your last . . . or it *may* lead you to fame and fortune!

Six levels below the White House lawn, in Annex U36, you lean back in the big red leather chair in the office of J.J. Obbard, director of the Special Intelligence Group. He glares at you through steel-rimmed glasses from behind a massive oak desk and taps his black briar pipe on the rim of a crystal bowl.

"Have you ever heard the sounds of the humpback whales?" Obbard asks you. "They're like organ music—beautiful and eerie."

"Uh huh," you reply.

Obbard picks up a letter from his desk. "From Dr. Claude DuMont in Boston to the President of the United States."

Dear Mr. President:

While tracking humpback whales near Bermuda last month, we recorded whalesongs of a type we have never heard before.

The whales have a secret, and the new whalesong is the key. We are analyzing it with our

computers. I'll advise you of our findings as soon
as possible.

> Respectfully yours,
> Claude DuMont
> Director, Center for
> Marine Studies

"If DuMont is correct," Obbard says, "it's important for us to learn the meaning of the new whalesong before anyone else does. For one thing, it will help us find where these whales go when they disappear."

"What do you mean?" you ask.

Obbard chews on his pipe before explaining. "At a time when there should be lots of humpback whales off Greenland, where they migrate to in the summer, they seem to disappear completely. Since they can only stay underwater for thirty minutes, we have a mystery. Where do they go?"

"Do you want me to go up to Boston and talk to DuMont?" you ask.

Obbard fastens his eyes upon you as he pauses to light his pipe. "I'm afraid your assignment will be more difficult than that," he says. "DuMont has been missing for thirty-six hours. We believe he has been kidnapped by KGB agents, led by someone known as 'Double-Eye.'"

Obbard pushes a folder across the desk. You pick it up and read a report of how, the day before last, DuMont met with Professor Hans Klein, who agreed to help prepare the computer program that would be used in studying the new whalesong. After the meeting, DuMont told Klein he was going straight home. He never made it.

"We've booked you on the next plane to Boston," Obbard says, as you put the report back on the desk. "A helicopter is waiting to take you to the airport. Find DuMont. Find the whalesong tape. Your mission is top priority. Your code name is *Jonah.*"

An hour and twenty minutes later, your 727 Stratojet touches down at Logan International Airport in Boston. You know that Dr. Hans Klein is a key man in the case. Perhaps you should see him first. On the other hand, the scientists at the Center for Marine Studies surely have been following DuMont's work closely. There is a good chance they have important information about the humpback whales.

If you visit Dr. Hans Klein, turn to page 4.

If you visit the Center for Marine Studies, turn to page 6.

4

Dr. Klein receives you at his ivy-covered brick house overlooking the Charles River in Cambridge. After checking your identity, he invites you into his study.

"DuMont was on the verge of a great discovery," he exclaims, as soon as you are both seated. "We were using my omputer to analyze the new whalesong, but I can't do it without DuMont. I'll be glad to play the tape for you."

The phone rings before you have a chance to reply. Klein answers it and beckons you over.

"It's Mr. Obbard calling from Washington."

"Sorry to bother you," Obbard says, "but this may be important. A Cessna 323 executive jet landed in Halifax an hour ago. On board was a KGB agent named Anton Roudnitska, who is posing as a businessman. He has been tracking DuMont, and we have been following him. He was met at the Halifax airport and driven to a seaside farmhouse. There's a motorboat anchored in the cove nearby. We're pretty sure that Roudnitska plans to use it to get to a Russian submarine. You may want to go up there right away. This may lead us to DuMont. You can catch the afternoon plane if you hurry."

If you stay and ask Klein to play the whalesong tapes, turn to page 7.

If you take the first plane to Halifax to track down Anton Roudnitska, turn to page 8.

If you go to the Boston FBI to check out their files on Dr. Claude DuMont, turn to page 9.

You take a taxicab to the center, a modest, two-story building on the Charles River, and are met by Dr. Miles Rueff, the assistant director. He tells you that although whales are highly intelligent animals, there is no evidence that they communicate in a complex fashion, as do human beings.

"Whalesongs are probably no different from birdsongs, except they are longer," Rueff says. "After all, whales have much bigger lungs."

Your conversation is interrupted by a phone call from Paul McKim, assistant to the president. McKim tells you that the president has received another letter from Dr. DuMont, but that it mysteriously disappeared before he had a chance to read it.

"You'd better get down here as quickly as possible," McKim says.

"You didn't call me by name," you reply.

There is a short pause.

"Sorry, Jonah," he replies.

You inform Dr. Rueff that you must leave for Washington, but he urges you to wait awhile in order to talk to Dr. Renata Carini, an Italian scientist who is expected at any moment.

"She knows a lot about what the Russians are doing," Dr. Rueff says. "I'm sure it will be worth your while to stay and talk to her."

If you leave immediately for Washington,
turn to page 12.

If you wait to talk to Dr. Carini,
turn to page 14.

"I want to hear that tape," you say.

Dr. Klein inserts a cassette into a player connected to an AIM 660 computer. In a moment, you hear the melodic piping of whales.

Klein holds up a hand.

"Listen," he says. "The new song is about to start."

You hear a clicking sound, then silence. Klein fiddles with the player and then turns and looks at you with a puzzled expression.

"Someone has erased the new whalesong," he exclaims. "How could this have happened? This room is locked at all times. The only other copy of the tape is at the computer center. We'd better get over there."

As Klein finishes speaking, the phone rings. He answers and hands it over to you.

"Jonah, this is Jim Keegan, FBI-Washington. Don Taylor, a British Intelligence agent, is in bad shape in the Provincetown Hospital. Someone ran him off the road. He has important information about the whalesong tape. I can't reach Obbard, but I advise you to get down there on the four o'clock plane. It's the last flight today."

Don Taylor may have the key to everything. On the other hand, one of the whalesong tapes has been erased. Maybe you'd better get to the other one, even if it means missing the plane to Provincetown.

If you tell Klein to take you out to the computer center, turn to page 16.

If you leave immediately for Provincetown, turn to page 17.

8

You promptly take leave of Klein, hail a cab, and head for the airport. It will be dark when you reach Halifax. You'll have to stay overnight in a hotel, rent a car, and head out to the farmhouse in the morning.

While waiting for your plane, you learn that a storm is expected. High winds and six- to eight-foot waves are predicted for the next couple of days—too rough for Roudnitska to put to sea. You'll have time to close in on him.

Turn to page 10.

The files at the Boston FBI office show that DuMont was esteemed and trusted by family, friends, and colleagues alike. Though no one had the slightest doubt as to his loyalty to America, everyone agreed that his greatest concern was for the rights of whales.

DuMont's closest associate at the Center for Marine Studies was Professor Harry Childers.

If you decide to talk to Professor Childers, turn to page 20.

If you decide to talk to Mrs. DuMont turn to page 22.

A few hours later, you land at Halifax airport, pick up your baggage, and walk outside into the cold, misty night.

As you wait for a cab to take you to the Lord Dunbar Hotel, a black Ford drives up. A well-tailored young woman steps out and walks up to you.

"Jonah?" She gestures with her hand, indicating that she wants you to get inside the car.

Obbard must have gotten in touch with the Canadian Intelligence Office and asked them to provide you with assistance. As you step forward to get in the car, you exchange glances with the driver, a heavyset man with a cap pulled down over his forehead. He smiles at you.

The woman knows your code name, so you have no reason to doubt that she is on your side. Yet, for some reason, you feel suspicious. Maybe you're just getting jumpy from being in this business so long.

If you get in the car, turn to page 24.

If you decide to step back and ask a few questions, turn to page 25.

As soon as you arrive at the White House, you are ushered into McKim's office.

A tall, gaunt man in his late forties, McKim relates to you that at about 9:30 yesterday morning Maria Bitner, the president's secretary, opened a new letter to the president from Dr. Claude Du-Mont. She put the letter on a table for the president to look at later that day. When she came back a half hour later, it was missing.

"Who had access to this room?" you ask McKim.

"Only the president, his security advisor—Henry Timbers—and myself, and, of course, Mrs. Bitner."

McKim rises as the president himself walks into the room. The two of you shake hands, and the president asks about your work on the case.

Go on to the next page.

"There are a number of mysteries about this," the president says, "the new whalesong, the disappearing whales, the disappearance of Dr. DuMont, and now the disappearance of his letter.

"I'd like you to stay right here until you can find out what happened to that letter. But Obbard tells me he has a plane waiting to take you to the *Arcturus,* a diesel schooner, chartered to monitor Russian experiments with the whales. The skipper reports there is a Russian spy on the *Arcturus* who has defected and is willing to turn over valuable information. We could get our own security people to check out this stolen letter business, unless you feel you should handle it yourself."

If you say, "I think I'd better find out what happened to DuMont's missing letter," turn to page 28.

If you say you want to leave for the Arcturus *immediately, turn to page 29.*

You wait impatiently for several hours until Renata Carini finally arrives. A slim, black-haired woman with olive skin and luminous dark eyes, she speaks flawless English.

"Claude DuMont is convinced that the whales have developed a language," she tells you.

"Do you think he's right?" you ask.

"I'm sure of it," she replies. "We have not been able to crack their code; they have cracked ours. They are able to speak to us, but they are not yet ready."

"What do you mean?"

"Suppose," she replies, "all-powerful beings from outer space are plundering the Earth and killing off most of the human population. They enter our atmosphere in spaceships that travel at the speed of light. We don't know the aliens' language so we can only broadcast a message in our own language and hope they understand it. What would you say?"

"I would have to give that some thought," you reply.

"Of course!" Carini says. "The whales have been giving it a lot of thought. But right now we must save Dr. DuMont."

"Do you have any idea how to do that?"

"Yes, I do," Carini replies. "The Russians will want to get DuMont aboard a Russian submarine. Their agent in charge of this is known as Double-Eye. He owns a villa at Truro on Cape Cod, and he has his own yacht."

"We must stop him," you respond.

"My XK3 Ferrari is waiting outside," she says.

You excuse yourself for a moment and telephone Obbard to get his thoughts.

"We think Carini is on the level," he replies, "but we just got a startling report from an informer in New York. The Russians are analyzing the whalesong tape in a brownstone house off Central Park occupied by a man named Ivan Ivenko. We are now sure that Ivenko is Double-Eye. Can you follow this up? You may be able to break this case wide open."

If you go with Dr. Carini to Truro, turn to page 31.

If you leave Carini and go instead to New York, turn to page 33.

"What sort of security do they have here?" you ask, as Klein drives you along the twisting streets of Cambridge in his old blue Mercedes.

"Just a uniformed guard and an internal alarm system," he replies.

In a few minutes, Klein pulls up in front of the two-story, windowless, gray granite building and parks about forty feet behind a maroon Buick. Suddenly, the Buick begins to back up. It slams its bumper against the Mercedes. Another car screeches to a stop right behind you. The Mercedes is wedged in, unable to move.

An electronically amplified voice calls, "Both of you get out of the car, hands up, or you'll go up in flames!"

You activate your radio distress beeper. You know the SIG helicopter is in the air within 10 miles of your car. It travels at 120 miles per hour, so there's a 50 percent chance it can reach you within 2½ minutes. The police would not be far behind.

If you say to Klein, "Let's stall a few minutes, I can get us some help," turn to page 34.

If you say, "We'd better go along with them," turn to page 78.

You tell Klein that Provincetown can't wait. You ask him to make sure the whalesong tape at the computer center is well guarded while you're away, and head for the airport.

Turn to page 18.

A few hours later, you are standing at the bed-
side of Don Taylor. Although he was badly shaken
up, with a concussion and two cracked ribs, the
doctors tell you that he will pull through all right.

Taylor looks up at you inquiringly.

"Tough break," you say.

"Who are you?" he asks.

"Call me Jonah," you reply.

"Thank heavens you're here," he says and
pauses to catch his breath. He is still in a good deal

of pain. "We discovered that the Russians set up a very sophisticated underwater listening equipment at Galey Point. They have a copy of DuMont's tape, and they're taking it out to a Russian sub by raft at dusk. They're using the abandoned lighthouse there . . ."

His voice trails off.

You glance out the window. The sun is almost setting. You have very little time. You have to get that tape.

If you head out to Galey Point alone, turn to page 36.

If you call the naval radar station in Truro for help, turn to page 40.

You find Professor Childers in his office in the Department of Linguistics. He is a small man with long, thin white hair brushed back on his head.

"It's tragic about DuMont's disappearance," Childers says. "He was one of the great scientists of our time. And I think he was on the verge of being able to talk to the whales."

"Could that really be possible?" you ask.

"Indeed, if the whales are ready to talk and we are ready to listen. But mind you they won't suddenly start saying 'cookie' or 'give me fish.' They may already be talking, and we are failing to understand them. They may already have a highly structured language, but you would have as much trouble understanding them as you would a recording of an ancient Egyptian speeded up to three times and played backward. Also, assume that words have different meanings depending on pitch and so forth. Also, assume the speaker has never been on land. Perhaps you begin to get my point?"

"Where do you think DuMont is?" you ask.

Childers pauses to stroke his chin before replying. "Well, I know that if the Russians succeeded in capturing him and tried to use him for communicating with the whales for their own purposes, he would try to protect the whales from them."

"Is there any chance he would have gone with them on purpose?" you ask.

"Look, my friend," Childers says. "What would you do?"

"I'm not here to speculate about what I would do," you reply. "I'm here to find out what DuMont did!"

"Yes," Childers replies, "and you seem to want my cooperation in that, but I still want to know what you would do if you were DuMont."

"You mean you'll only tell the truth if I pass your test?" you ask.

"I am an old man," Childers says. "I follow my conscience. I have nothing to fear from governments."

"I see," you reply. "Very well then. I would do nothing to harm the whales."

"Ah," Childers replies. "Then you have no need to interview me."

You are puzzled and dismayed by Childers' behavior. Why does he choose to talk in riddles? You bid him good-by and return to your car. Before you get there, you feel a jabbing pressure in your back. You tilt back. A rope flips over your head and around your neck—then a blow falls on your head.

Turn to page 26.

When you knock on the door of the modest white house in Cambridge where Dr. DuMont and his wife have made their home for the past forty years, you are greeted by a small, elderly lady with sparkling blue eyes.

"I've been expecting you, Jonah," she says. "Won't you come in?"

As Mrs. DuMont shows you into her husband's study, you express condolences over his disappearance and say that you hope to be able to find him quickly.

"Please sit down," she says abruptly. "Before you ask me any questions, I have one for you."

"Just one," you reply, "for I have no time to spare."

"I think one would be enough," she answers.

"You are hired to work for the Special Intelligence Group. They pay you for your work. But I want to know what strikes you as the most important thing about the new whalesong?"

If you reply, ". . . that it could mean a threat and an opportunity for the United States," turn to page 42.

If you reply, ". . . that this could be a very important event in the history of man," turn to page 43.

You step into the back of the car. Suddenly, a man you hadn't noticed before gets in next to you. The opposite door opens. You wheel around and see another man with a black hat pulled down over his forehead. They have you boxed in. Each of them is pointing a snub-nosed revolver at you. You slide into the middle of the backseat. The woman gets in front. The car speeds off. You feel a heavy blow on your head.

Turn to page 26.

You step back and study the woman closely. Out of the corner of your eye, you notice a man in a black raincoat approaching. You whirl and run toward the entrance to the airport, then dash for a taxi and jump in.

"Take me to the Lord Dunbar Hotel," you tell the driver.

He accelerates down the airport access road, while you watch out the rear window. The Ford is following.

"Can you shake that car behind us?" you ask.

"I don't know, but I'll give it a try—I've always liked a good race."

He accelerates and then makes a screaming turn, doubling back on a side road. You hear the screeching of brakes behind you as the Ford tries to stay on your tail.

Your car gathers speed.

"If we can cross McCurdy Avenue before the light changes, they'll never get us," the driver says.

You glance at the speedometer; it's quivering at 65 MPH. The light is changing; McCurdy Avenue is about a hundred yards away. Now the light is yellow. A car ahead of you is braking to a stop. The black Ford is gaining from behind. Cross traffic is beginning to move as the light changes. You don't see how your driver can make the crossing, but that may be your only chance.

If you tell the driver to gun it,
turn to page 46.

If you tell him to brake,
turn to page 50.

You are awakened by bright sunlight shining on your face. You are lying in an old-fashioned, iron-frame bed. Through the window you can see cows grazing in the distance. There's no chance to escape; your ankle is chained to the bedstead.

While you lie there, rubbing your throbbing head, two short, stocky thugs enter the room. They are almost comically similar—with crude, puffy faces and slicked-back, greasy hair.

While one of them covers you with a snub-nosed pistol, the other unchains you and forces you up out of bed. They lead you to another room and seat you at a table next to a telephone.

"In a moment that phone will ring," one of them says. "The person calling will be Dr. Claude Du-Mont. You will identify yourself so that he will know it is really you he is talking to. Then you will tell him that the only way the whales can be saved now is to get Russian cooperation."

"So you think this will trick DuMont into talking?" you ask sarcastically.

"That's right," the thug remarks, "we have other ways, of course. Using you is our *humane* method." He laughs. "But if you play any tricks, you will die." The phone rings.

If you refuse to cooperate,
turn to page 91.

If you say you'll cooperate,
hoping somehow to warn DuMont,
turn to page 94.

"I think that while I'm here, Mr. President, I'd better talk to the people who had access to that letter," you say.

"Fine," he replies. "I'm sure McKim will give you all the help you need."

After the president leaves, you exchange glances with McKim. He has a kindly face but seems very nervous; he must be under a lot of stress.

Turn to page 49.

Six hours have passed. You have just been dropped by helicopter on the deck of the schooner, *Arcturus*. Captain Lindstrom is briefing you on the progress of his mission.

"We have wonderful tapes of the new whalesong," the captain says, "but we haven't been able to decipher it. They're working on it at MIT, you know."

"What about the Russian defector?" you ask.

"Ah, yes," Lindstrom replies. "We have on board Alexi Minkov, who deserted from a Russian submarine. He has told us that he has a secret but he doesn't feel ready to tell yet. He says that, although he has defected from Russia, he still loves his country and has a certain loyalty to it. I respect that. I respect him because he is honest and sees that everything is not simple."

Lindstrom is interrupted by amplified melodic sounds coming from the monitoring station.

"Those are real whales you're listening to," he says, "not just recordings. But that's an old song. We think it means *gather here*. They're only a few hundred yards away."

Go on to the next page.

The two of you pick up binoculars in hopes of catching a glimpse of the whales, but a thick fog has been closing in, and at the moment you can only see a hundred feet or so.

Suddenly, you hear a thumping sound from the sound scanner.

"It's a sub," the captain exclaims, "a Russian sub."

"This may be a chance for a rendezvous," he says, "a meeting at the summit of the waves; or it may mean we will be destroyed. What do you think we should do?"

If you say, "sail toward them,"
turn to page 100.

If you say, "sail away—we must escape,"
turn to page 102.

Renata Carini maneuvers through traffic like a veteran race-car driver. In a few minutes you approach the highway to Cape Cod.

"You think you know where Dr. DuMont is being held—how do you propose to contact him?" you ask.

"You must realize," she says, "that DuMont and I are experts in communication. We each carry a miniaturized, ultrasonic communicator that is inaudible to human ears."

You nod and study the map while she concentrates on pressing the Ferrari to its limits.

By the time you approach your destination, darkness has set in, but Carini seems sure of herself as she cuts through dirt roads and through the scrubby brush, skidding wildly as the Ferrari barrels through sand that has drifted onto the road.

"Take it easy," you say. "If we get stuck in the sand, your 300-horsepower engine won't do us any good."

"I work best walking a tightrope," she replies.

A few seconds later she screeches around a sharp curve and pulls the car off the road onto hard ground.

"I used to come here in the summer for vacation," she says. "I know these sandy roads, the freshwater ponds, the paths to the blueberry bushes and the dunes, the beaches, the pebbles on the beaches—the whole business."

"Where do we go from here?" you ask.

"We'll follow this path. We'll soon be able to see the lights of the house. Then I'll activate my ultrasonic communicator."

Go on to the next page.

The two of you make your way through the brush for a hundred yards or so by flashlight until you see the lights of a house ahead.

"Shh. . . . We're close enough," Carini says. "Now I can find out whether DuMont is there."

She holds the communicator in the palm of her hand, extends a tiny antenna, and taps out a silent message.

You stand next to her, skeptical, wondering.

"We're transmitting. I've raised the intensity, even though you can't hear it," she says.

In a moment you hear an answering response on the communicator, but it is quickly drowned out by the barking and growling of dogs coming at you from the house.

"That's the trouble with these things," she says. "People can't hear them, but dogs can. At least we know DuMont is in there, but those dogs will be here in a moment."

"They may be attack dogs," you say. "What shall we do?"

Suddenly two large German shepherds are coming right at you. Carini activates her communicator. She is able to hold them at bay for the moment by directing high-intensity ultrasonic vibrations at them. The dogs whine with pain. You hear voices from near the house.

If you tell Carini to run with you back to the safety of the Ferrari, turn to page 55.

If you tell her to keep the dogs at bay, while you circle around and try to surprise the KGB agents, turn to page 56.

When you get off the plane in New York, you are met by a courier with a note from Obbard:

> We think Double-Eye is a man named Ivan Ivenko, but we don't know how to prove it. For the past three months only a few people have ever entered or left his 73rd Street brownstone house; yet a lot must go on there, because Consolidated Edison reports billing Ivenko over $7,500 each month just for electricity. We have a hunch the whalesong tape is in that house. Get it.

You have to think of a way to get into Ivenko's house. You could pretend to be willing to sell him information about the whalesongs. You know enough so that you could probably convince him you are worth talking to. Or, you might try a somewhat more unorthodox method—firing your Mark MX high intensity smokebomb into an open window. The Mark MX bomb emits dense synthetic smoke, which drives occupants out of a building. In the confusion it should be fairly easy to get inside.

If you try to gain entrance by posing as an informant, turn to page 64.

If you try to gain entrance by using the Mark MX smokebomb, turn to page 66.

"Let's sit tight for a minute," you tell Klein. As you are speaking, you smell a strange odor.

"They're gassing us through the ventilation system," Klein cries.

You hold your breath, knowing you will have to open the car door and get out within a few seconds. Klein has his hand on the door handle. You hear the whirring sound of a helicopter, then police sirens. Klein's door opens. Coughing from the acrid smoke, you dive out the door. The Buick is going up in flames.

Keeping low, you run for safety. Klein is right behind you.

"Some business you're in," he says.

The helicopter is now on the ground, surrounded by police cars. You and Klein cautiously return to the scene.

"We won that round, but we haven't seen the last of them," Klein says.

A few hours later, while you're back in your hotel resting, the phone rings.

It's Obbard. "What are you sitting around there for?" he asks. "I want you to follow up that Halifax lead."

Turn to page 10.

You rush out of the hospital and into your rented Triumph BR-50 coupe. Getting the whalesong tape from ruthless espionage agents will not be easy, but you were not hired to do easy jobs.

You roar across the Cape at high speed. Traffic is light. Within ten minutes, the Triumph is climbing along the high ridge leading to Galey Point. You can look down at a field of marsh grass, beyond which lies the great salt pond. At the end of a dirt road going off to your left is an abandoned lighthouse. A red Datsun pickup truck and two small cars are parked nearby. The sun is just above the horizon, and darkness will soon be setting in. With your Quasar high-revolution spotting scope, you scan the path leading down to the dunes that rim the shore, then examine the area around the lighthouse. You can see a blue-green rubber raft in the pickup truck. You know that rubber rafts are always yellow or orange so they can be spotted easily from the air. It's not hard to imagine why this one is not.

You drive on a short distance, pull the Triumph off the road, and park it behind some scrub cedar, where it will be hidden from view, then make your way through the brush.

Turn to page 38.

Using the setting sun as your compass, you make your way to the beach and walk along it until you spot the trail leading up through the dunes to the barn. Then you wait in the shelter of the tall grass. You have only been there a few minutes when you see three men carrying the raft down to the water. They launch it through the surf and begin to paddle toward the reef.

You assemble your RR-13 rifle. One shot through the rubber raft would send it and the stolen whalesong tape to the bottom. The agents could swim to shore—it would be a satisfactory result.

On the other hand, there is a Marlin 475-horsepower 26-foot cruiser tied up to the dock. You could take it and capture the spies and retrieve the tape—with a little luck.

*If you try to sink the raft,
turn to page 82.*

*If you try to take the boat,
turn to page 84.*

You rush to the phone and dial the NAS hotline.

"Nicholson here," a crisp voice answers.

"This is Jonah," you reply. "Priority 1. Need helicopter and CE force 3 immediately. Can you pick me up by helicopter at the hospital?"

"One moment, please," the voice replies coolly, "checking your code name. Is this SIG directive?"

"Look, this is urgent," you reply. "If you're not classified for this, get me someone who is. We have only minutes to spare."

"OK, hold on," the voice replies.

You hear a commotion at the other end; then another voice comes on.

"Hello, who is this?"

"This is Jonah," you say impatiently.

"Jonah, this is Lieutenant Gascoyne, the OD."

"Can you get a helicopter and CE force 3 to the hospital at once?" you shout into the phone.

"Hold on," Gascoyne replies.

You wait for what seems like hours, looking alternately at your watch and the darkening sky.

"Sorry, Jonah," Gascoyne says. "Our helicopter is in the shop. We have a car on the way to the hospital to pick you up. Be there in half a minute."

You wait impatiently. Finally, a gray Dodge sedan with three marines in it screeches to a halt. You run out and jump in. The car accelerates rapidly and careens through the narrow streets of Provincetown. A few minutes later, you are on the road to Galey Point.

The marines look grim and determined. As you approach the ridge along the ocean, you discuss whether to storm the lighthouse or try to stay undercover. The driver brakes sharply as you approach a curve. Suddenly, you hear shots. The car careens crazily off the road and crashes through the thick brush to a trembling stop.

"They shot out two tires!" the driver shouts.

One of the agents radios for help, but you know you've failed in your mission. By the time you can reach Galey Point, the whalesong tape will be far below the ocean waves—inside a Russian submarine.

A few months later you find out how your adversaries knew you were in the car. Don Taylor was only posing as a British agent. His real employer was the KGB.

The End

"Ah," Mrs. DuMont replies, "threat and opportunity—the creed of the day. Opportunity for what, I ask—to turn the oceans into your playground? Slaughtering whales is not enough; so you will enslave them?"

You start to protest, but she holds up one hand to keep you from speaking.

"I will tell you this much," she continues heatedly. "When Dr. DuMont learned the secret of the whales, he became concerned that the Russians would take from the whales what is rightly theirs."

"I believe in conserving endangered species," you say. "Whales are wonderful creatures. But I am much more concerned with the future of the human race—and that, I'm afraid, depends a great deal on the strength of America."

"Don't misunderstand me," Mrs. DuMont replies. "I'm more interested in human beings than in whales. My point is that unless we save the whales we may lose ourselves."

You respect Mrs. DuMont's views, but you can see there is little to be gained by talking to her further. You bid her good day and hail a taxi. It's time to visit the Center for Marine Studies.

Turn to page 6.

"I'm glad you feel that way," Mrs. DuMont says. "I believe I can trust you, so I will tell you the truth. The new whalesong is a message. Its meaning is this: the whales have discovered a great cavern in Deception Island, off Greenland. The cavern can only be approached underwater. Once inside, the whales rise up to sea level to breathe. The cavern may be as much as twenty kilometers across, and its roof a hundred meters above the surface of the water. It's dark, of course, but the whales can, in effect, 'see' with sound waves. This haven, perhaps, has kept them from extinction. It is their homeland. It would also make a submarine base that could be invulnerable to attack.

"If DuMont is captured, he will do everything he can to keep this knowledge from the Russians. He has also decided to keep it from the United States Government. I don't know whether he is right or wrong, but I have decided to trust you—and to trust your judgment."

You thank Mrs. DuMont and bid her good-by. As soon as you get back to your hotel, you telephone Obbard.

If you report your conversation with Mrs. DuMont to Obbard, turn to page 88.

If you decide to keep it secret, turn to page 89.

You just can't seem to make much progress in your investigation. The president is unavailable, so you report back to Obbard.

"I guess you're better out in the field where the action is," he says. "Well, here's an assignment you may like! A well-known computer expert named Ivan Ivenko owns a brownstone house on West 73rd Street in New York City. Some of his employees live and work in the house. They have very sophisticated radio and computer equipment that seems to consume a great deal of electricity. We can't be sure, but we think Ivan Ivenko is Double-Eye. He may have a copy of the whalesong tape. I want you to get inside that house. You ought to be able to convince him you have something he wants to buy."

"I'm on my way," you reply.

And a few hours later you step out of a taxi in front of Ivan Ivenko's house.

Turn to page 64.

"Beat the light!" you shout.

The driver steps on the gas, racing through the intersection against the red light. You see a huge gray truck bearing down. It tries to swerve.

"Watch it!" you shout.

The driver turns sharply. The truck roars by, catching the back of your car and sending it into a terrifying spin. You double up on the floor. In the instant before blacking out, you are flung wildly against the front seat.

The moment you wake up, you know you are in a hospital, and that you've been here for quite a while, because J.J. Obbard is looking down at you. Your cabdriver is standing next to him, his arm in a sling and a bandage around his head.

"Sorry, Jonah, it looks like you're out of the operation," Obbard says. "Take it easy and get well. We'll need you again before long, I'm sure. By the way, you haven't been introduced to your cabdriver—Anton Roudnitska."

You look up with surprise at the smiling, bandaged man.

"He's really working for us," Obbard says. "Thank the Lord."

A nurse walks into the room. "Sorry," she says. "The patient has to rest."

"We'll tell you what happened when you're feeling better," Obbard says.

He waves good-by and beckons Roudnitska to come with him.

You realize you need a lot more rest, and in a few minutes you are asleep, listening in a dream to the haunting songs of the humpback whales.

The End

You return to McKim's office and close the door behind you.

"Did you figure out who took DuMont's letter?" he asks.

"Yes, you!"

"Who? Wha—me? Why, that's preposterous," he replies.

"No, it's not. It has to be you, because if Mrs. Bitner had taken the letter she never would have reported it missing. And, since she is innocent, we can assume she was telling the truth when she said that two other letters were never taken from under the ashtray. Yet you were so anxious to show that DuMont's letter had been taken before you got there that you insisted that there were *no* letters under the ashtray."

McKim doesn't blink an eye. Instead, he reaches in his desk, pulls out a letter, and shows it to you.

"Since you want to know what DuMont said in that letter, here it is," he says.

"You mean you took this letter before the president could see it?" you reply.

"Read it," McKim says.

You glance at the handwriting. DuMont wrote it, all right. The letter reads:

Dear Mr. President:

I have discovered the new whalesong is a signal telling where the whales disappear to—an enormous underwater cavern under Deception Island, off the east coast of Greenland.

I will be happy to discuss this with you. Meanwhile, I urge that the cavern of the whales be preserved as their rightful property.

Respectfully yours,
Claude DuMont

"I'm the one who stole the letter," McKim says, as you finish reading it. "I did so because DuMont called me and asked me to intercept it, saying he had decided that he did not want the president to know about the cavern of the whales."

"And you are withholding this information even though the president is elected to make the decision?" you ask.

"I have to follow my conscience," McKim says. "Now you'll have to follow yours."

If you say, "My conscience says we must go to the president immediately and tell him everything," turn to page 54.

If you say, "I'll have to think about this, and let my conscience be my guide," turn to page 114.

"Do you feel that either Mrs. Bitner or Secretary Timbers took the letter?" you ask McKim

"Logically, one of them must have taken it," he replies, "but they have both stood up under every conceivable security investigation."

"Were you in Mrs. Bitner's office between 9:30 and 10:00, when she claims she returned and found the letter missing from under the ashtray?" you ask.

"Yes, I came looking for her a few minutes before 10:00. She wasn't there, so I left."

"Did you notice anything?"

"Well, I did notice that her desk was clear and there was no letter under the ashtray."

If you decide to question Mrs. Bitner,
turn to page 52.

If you decide to question Timbers,
turn to page 53.

If you decide to give up trying to
find who took the letter, turn to page 44.

"Brake!" you yell.

The driver brakes and swerves. The car careens to a stop against an embankment. The front, right fender crumples against a rock outcropping.

You glance back and see the Ford barreling over a concrete wall. Seconds later it explodes with a roar in a ravine below.

You thank your driver for his work. Strangely, he just smiles and says, "Any time."

Early the next morning, after a few hours' sleep at the Lord Dunbar Hotel, you rent a car and drive out to the farmhouse.

You park off the road a quarter of a mile from the farmhouse and cut through the scrub woods until you find a place from which you can observe without being seen.

Two approaches seem possible. An attic window is open. With your Mark 3K harpoon gun, you can shoot a line inside. Your line has a grapple on it, which will hook under the window when you pull. Then you can climb up the wall and into the attic and eavesdrop on everything going on in the house.

Another option is to knock on the front door and pretend you are one of their own agents.

If you attempt to enter through the attic, turn to page 96.

If you attempt to bluff your way in, turn to page 98.

You and Mrs. Bitner sit down in her office.

"Tell me what happened," you say.

"An aide brought me several letters at about 9:20," Mrs. Bitner replies. "I screened them quickly to see which ones were important enough for the president. I knew he would want to read the letter from DuMont, so I put it under the ashtray along with a couple of others that looked important. I left for a meeting at 9:30. When I came back at 10:00 the other two letters were there, but DuMont's was missing."

If you haven't talked to Timbers and decide to question him, turn to page 53.

If you have talked to Timbers and decide to question McKim further, turn to page 47.

If you decide to give up trying to find out who took the letter, turn to page 44.

Timbers ushers you into his office and gestures toward a chair. He seems somewhat nervous but not unfriendly.

"Were you in Mrs. Bitner's office between 9:30 and 10:00 when she claims she returned and found the letter missing from under the ashtray?" you ask.

"Yes, I came in just after 9:30 looking for her. She wasn't there, so I left."

"Did you notice anything?"

"Not a thing."

"Did you notice whether there was anything under the ashtray?" you persist.

"I really didn't even notice whether there *was* an ashtray. I just glanced around the room and left."

"Thank you, Mr. Timbers."

If you haven't talked to Mrs. Bitner and decide to question her, turn to page 52.

If you have talked to Mrs. Bitner and decide to question McKim further, turn to page 47.

If you decide to give up trying to find who took the letter, turn to page 44.

"Good," says McKim. "And don't worry about that letter. The president has already seen it! We have been testing your fitness for the job, and you're doing fine. You'll also be glad to know the case is closed. We've reached an agreement with the Russians. DuMont has been returned home safely. The whales will be protected and their cavern kept off limits for military and commercial purposes."

You walk out of McKim's office with a smile on your face, feeling as light as a whale in the water.

The End

You and Carini retreat to the Ferrari. The dogs hesitate at first, stunned by the ultrasonic blasts. Then they charge the car, barking and growling angrily in frustration.

"We can turn this to our advantage," Carini says. "I'll drive away slowly. The dogs will follow. The agents will start down the road, wondering where their dogs are going. You go in the house, free DuMont, and lead him south along the beach, and I'll pick you up about a mile down the beach."

*If you agree to this plan,
turn to page 57.*

*If instead you insist upon going into
town and calling Obbard for instructions,
turn to page 58.*

While Carini holds off the dogs with ultrasonic pulses, you circle around through the brush. You hear the dogs howling and whining as they follow the car, and then a man shouting in some Slavic language.

You soon reach the lawn behind the house. In the fading light of the moon, you can see the path leading down to the beach.

There is a sliding glass door at the back of the house, which leads to the lower level. You try it and find it locked. You slip a jackknife blade into the handle and pry the door open enough to jam in a power wedge from your entry kit. In a moment you are inside.

You hear voices from upstairs; the lower level is dark and silent. You sweep your insta-flood lamp around the main room. There are sofas, a television, and at the far corner, a large pool table. You walk into a hall, which leads to several rooms with closed doors. You try the first one. It is locked, but a voice from within calls, "Yes, what is it?"

If you say softly, "Is that you, DuMont?"
turn to page 60.

If you step a little further down
the hall and wait to see what happens,
turn to page 62.

You find your way around to the back of the house and shine your flashlight through a dark window. The light shines full on DuMont. He is strapped to a chair. You get inside through the back door, cut his bonds, escort him out into the backyard, then point to the path leading to the beach.

"I've no time to explain," you say. "Please—go down the path. When you get to the beach, turn left. After half a mile you will reach Pamet Point Road. Renata Carini will be waiting to pick you up."

"Thank you . . . thank you," DuMont says.

You watch for a moment as he disappears into the night; then you turn to the house, hoping you can now find the whalesong tape.

You head upstairs and start into the living room. A shot rings out. You fall to the floor. It's all over for you. At least you freed DuMont. You've been a good agent.

The End

"Too much risk," you tell Carini. "We need to get help. Take me into town. I want to call Obbard."

"You shouldn't be in this business," Carini says. "You don't have the stomach for it."

She accelerates down the dirt road, then onto Pamet Point Road, to the Blue Hill Tavern. You go inside and get Obbard on the phone.

"Stay where you are," he says. "We'll have three agents with you in half an hour. You need help for this operation, and make sure Dr. Carini stays put. We can't have any amateur in this."

As you step out of the phone booth, Carini is standing there smiling, a PPK-3 snub-nosed pistol in her hand.

"Now that your Mr. Obbard is *sure* that I'm an amateur, he'll never suspect that I take my orders from Moscow," she says smugly.

She fires, but you are already diving for her ankles and tackle her as she tries to break her fall. You wrench her PPK-3 pistol out of her hand, and in a moment you have her handcuffed.

"Quite a catch," Obbard says later. "It never occurred to us that Double-Eye was a woman!"

The End

When you call out DuMont's name, there is a moment of silence. Then a voice responds excitedly.

"Yes, who is it?"

You hear another voice from upstairs—this one in a broken accent—"Hey, who's down there? Ivan, get back here and get those dogs here!"

You have to act fast.

"Stand away," you shout. You draw your PPK 9-mm and shoot off the lock. You kick the door open and shine your insta-flood lamp onto the

startled face of Claude DuMont. He is tied to a chair, and you quickly cut him free.

"Special Intelligence Group. Follow me," you say.

He seems stunned, and you have to take his arm, lead him out, and point toward the glass door. At the same time, you hear footsteps on the stairs.

If you tell DuMont to escape by himself while you hold off the enemy agents, turn to page 68.

If you decide to surrender rather than risk DuMont's life in a shoot-out, turn to page 70.

DuMont may be in that room, but you decide to hide and let the enemy agents come to you, rather than expose yourself, so you cautiously explore the hallway. At the end is a utility room and workshop.

You hear voices and the sound of footsteps descending the stairs. In a moment you can tell they are opening the door to DuMont's room.

"All right, Comrade DuMont," a voice says. "It's time for you to go on a sea voyage."

Through the crack in the doorway you watch two men start to lead DuMont upstairs. There is no way to capture them without endangering his life.

You cautiously follow them up the stairs. The living room looks like the staging area for an amphibious assault. There are two rubber rafts, packs of equipment and food, and several automatic weapons. Suddenly, you see an opportunity— DuMont is separated from the agents. You run into the room, your auto-rifle at the ready.

"Don't any of you move" you shout.

Keeping an eye on your prisoners, you call the local police, the FBI, and then Obbard. You wait tensely, then breathe a sigh of relief as you hear the shrill wail of sirens. Within a minute and a half, the police have taken the enemy agents in custody. It looks as if you can get some rest for a change.

You are about to leave with DuMont and return to Boston, when the phone rings. It's Obbard.

"The president wants both of you to come to Washington immediately," he tells you.

You arrive at the White House early the next morning. The president greets you with a warm smile and a vigorous handshake.

"I have good news for you, Professor DuMont,"

he says. "I've been on the phone with the Soviet premier. We have agreed that the cavern has very limited military value and that we will negotiate a treaty providing that it will forever be reserved for the whales. I am appointing you, Professor, as chairman of a commission to draft the proposed treaty, and thus set the rules for protection of the whales."

The next thing you know, some TV cameramen are filming you shaking hands with the president. Someone else is playing the new whalesong on a tape player. It's beautiful music.

The End

You knock on the door. There is no response. You knock again. Finally, the door opens a few inches. A thick chain prevents it from opening further. A short, bulky man in a black suit and black tie peers out at you.

"What do you want?" he asks gruffly.

"I have some information that Ivan Ivenko wants very much. I am prepared to sell it for $10,000."

"I see," the black-suited man replies. "And what is the nature of this information?"

"It is the meaning of the new whalesong."

"Wait," the voice says, and the door slams in your face.

A few minutes later a tall woman opens the door. Her thick, reddish-blond hair is swept back tightly over her head.

"You may come in," she says in an icy voice.

The woman shows you into a lavishly furnished study, where a round-faced, bald man is seated at a large mahogany desk. He does not move, except to gesture toward a chair. You take a seat, quite sure that the man and the woman behind you have weapons pointed at your head.

"Are you Ivan Ivenko?" you ask.

"Just call me Double-Eye," the bald man replies. "Before I can pay you, I must trust you, right? Before I can trust you, you must trust me, right? If you trust me, you will state your code name. If you give a fake name, you will be liquidated. If you give your true name, I will place $10,000 in your hands. Then you will tell us the meaning of the new whalesong—the precise meaning. Incidentally, we already know your code name, so you have nothing to lose by revealing it."

"Since you haven't said my code name," you reply, "how do I know you really know it?"

"You can't be sure, it is true. But you won't want to take a chance on that, will you? *Come now, out with it!*"

If you say, "Call me Jonah,"
turn to page 72.

If you make up a fake code name,
turn to page 74.

You notice that a second-story window of the brownstone is wide open. You won't even have to break any glass. You take your portable launcher out of your dispatch case, insert a tiny explosive charge, take aim, and fire. Almost immediately, smoke begins to billow out of the window. You know that the Mark MX synthetic smoke will spread rapidly throughout the house.

You observe from a few steps away. In a moment a window opens, then the front door. Smoke is billowing out as if the whole house were on fire.

You see a man dressed in a black suit come running out. He looks around nervously. Then a tall woman with frizzy blond hair follows. A fat, bald man comes out, then a barrel-chested thug dressed in a sweatsuit. Everyone is looking down the street. Fire engines are already approaching. A crowd begins to gather.

You put on your smoke mask and slip inside the house. With your yellow-beam light, you are able to make your way upstairs, where the smoke is already clearing up. You throw another bomb down the stairs to delay anyone from entering. Then you look around on the second floor. It is divided into two large rooms. One of them is filled with electronic equipment.

It takes you only a couple of minutes to find the tape player and the tape itself, but when you reach the hall again, you see a sweatsuited thug coming up the stairs.

"I'll get you," he cries.

You whirl around a corner and run up the next flight of stairs, clutching the tape at your side. You throw open a door and step out onto the roof. You look over the edge. It's three stories down to the pavement, but there is a huge pile of garbage bags in the alley. A shot rings out. You don't have time to think. You jump.

You land in the heap of garbage—shaken but with no broken bones. You climb down and run out of the alley into the street. There is a taxi nearby, and you throw open the door and dive inside. Keeping very low, you tell the driver to take you to La Guardia Airport. Three hours later, you are seated once again in Obbard's office in Washington.

"Good work," he says. "You got the tape and the information needed for us to break up the biggest spy ring in the country."

The End

"Go to your left down the beach," you tell DuMont. "Renata Carini will pick you up where Bound Brook Road hits the beach. It's about a mile. Hurry!"

DuMont is surprisingly agile for his age, and you are relieved to see him taking off toward the beach at a good pace.

Now you turn your attention toward the stairs. You know the enemy agents may charge you at any moment. Suddenly, a bright searchlight is shining through a window. You crouch just inside the room where DuMont was locked up, so the light won't shine directly on you. Shots ring out. They are firing from the stairs and from the window. You return the fire. You've got to hold them off long enough for DuMont to get away.

Silence. What are they waiting for? You hear the dogs growling. They must have given up following Carini. Now you hear them on the stairs.

*If you vault out the window
and run for it, turn to page 76.*

*If you stand your ground,
turn to page 75.*

"We surrender," you call out.

"Very well," a thick-accented voice calls down the stairs. "March up, one at a time. Hands straight up over your heads . . . DuMont first."

You motion to DuMont, and he raises his hands and starts up the stairs. You throw down your weapon and prepare to follow.

"Very good," one of the agents says after the other has frisked you and DuMont. "So we have pulled in another fish. And, Victor, this is Jonah, is it not? You are surprised we know your code name—such an unlikely name for you. Yes . . . we know all about you. Well, Jonah, you are going to be swallowed by a whale."

He cackles at his little joke.

The agents bind, gag, and blindfold you. Later they take you and DuMont for a ride, then march you down a wooden ramp. You can smell a mixture of salt air and gasoline. Now you are boarding a boat.

Go on to the next page.

After a three-hour ride, you are transferred to a larger vessel. Finally, you are seated. Your blindfold and ropes are removed. You rub your eyes and look around. Sitting next to you is Claude DuMont, and, at the opposite side of the table, three Russian naval officers. The captain—a swarthy, pleasant-looking man—is standing at the far end of the table. He looks at you and says nothing for a moment.

"Feel right at home," he finally says. "Here, have some—how do you say?—Pepsi Cola, or would you prefer some Russian soup? And meet Captain Lindstrom, captain of a foundering sailing vessel, from which we rescued him. After going to all this trouble, causing you quite some inconvenience, I am sure, it turns out we didn't need to invite you here after all."

Turn to page 104.

"Very good, Jonah," the bald man says.

He spreads out a handful of thousand-dollar bills in front of you, There are ten of them.

"Now . . ." he says.

"The meaning is complex," you say. "I need to translate as I listen to the tape. Play the tape and I will translate it for you."

"Very well. It no longer matters that you know we have the tape. You came along at a very good time, you see. We found out you are the key U.S. agent on the case just about the time we found out that our computers would not be able to decode the whalesong."

The bald man picks up an intercom and says a few words in Russian. A few moments later, the tall woman wheels in a cart on which is mounted a tape player, speakers, and some other instruments.

Go on to the next page.

In a moment, you hear the eerie and beautiful sounds of the new whalesong. Now, you have what you want—the enemy agents and the stolen whalesong tape. The only problem is that there are two pistols pointed at the back of your head.

There hardly seems to be any choice; you must bluff your way through it somehow. You don't know the meaning of the new whalesong, but you know you have to pretend you do, and if you fail, then . . .

"Well, let's have the answers," the bald man snaps at you.

*If you say the whalesong means
"Warning, keep away from ships,"
turn to page 81.*

*If you say the whalesong means,
"Follow me to our secret place,"
turn to page 106.*

"Call me Whitecap," you say.

"Tsk, tsk," the bald man says. "It looks as if we can't count on you for anything, Jonah, *so we'll have to count you out.*"

Those are the last words you ever hear.

The End

For a long while there is silence. Are they preparing to attack or are they just conducting a war of nerves? You take a few steps down the hall, feeling along the wall. Your hand brushes against a doorknob. You open it and shine your insta-flood on a stocky man. There is a shining black shape in his hand. Standing next to him is Renata Carini!

"It's a pity," she says. "I enjoyed your company, but now that you know I'm really working for Moscow . . ."

The End

You jump out the window and run through the scrub woods, exchanging fire with enemy agents. They pursue you as you run toward the dunes. The dogs are closing in on you. You're out of ammunition. You jump down to the beach from a high dune. Looking back over your shoulder, you see the two attack dogs leaping through the air.

Your only hope is to run into the water and swim. The water is icy but, with no other choice, you plunge in and swim for your life. Once out away from shore, you numbly turn and swim along the beach. You can hear the dogs howling at the water's edge.

You can't keep it up. You are going to freeze.

There to your right is the green running light of a boat. You call for help. It veers toward you.

"Help!" you shout again.

In a moment they pull you aboard—two lobster fishermen. By now, you are in shock. Later, you wake up in a hospital bed, weak and exhausted. A doctor is standing over you.

"I've got to get out of here," you say.

"Forget it," she replies, smiling. "You have viral pneumonia, a temperature of 103, and a telegram from your boss giving you a six-week leave of absence."

You smile at her and go back to sleep.

The End

As you and Klein get out, two well-dressed men carrying attaché cases approach from the car in front of you. One of them is short with bristly gray hair. The other is slim and wears a neatly trimmed moustache. They cover you and Klein with automatic PPK-3 pistols while two thugs from the other car relieve you of your weapons.

The two well-dressed men march you and Klein into the computer center. The security guard gives Klein a friendly greeting, which turns into a cry of horror as he realizes Klein's colleagues are pointing guns at him. One of the foreign agents binds and gags the guard with the efficiency of a professional, while you and Klein watch helplessly.

"Take us to the whalesong tape," the short man says, "and make sure you deactivate any alarm, or we'll deactivate you—permanently."

Klein looks at you with fear in his eyes.

"Dr. Klein, lead our friends to the tapes," you say.

As the enemy agents march you into the building, you have a chance to whisper to Klein.

If you tell him to pretend to cooperate, but give them one of the old whalesong tapes, turn to page 79.

If you tell him to just hand over the new tape as they ask, turn to page 80.

Following your advice, Klein gives them the wrong tape. He puts on a good act, but the others see through it. That's the end of Klein—and you.

The End

Klein hands over the cassette. The KGB agents quickly check it on the player, smiling with satisfaction at what they hear.

"Let's tie them up," one of the agents says.

"No, we don't have time. It's simpler just to shoot them," the other says.

"No, comrade, that violates our instructions— only in special cases, remember?"

Their argument is interrupted by the sound of police sirens. The KGB men turn and run, slamming the doors behind them.

A minute later they are in the hands of the police. Soon you are on the phone again, reporting back to Obbard.

"Good work," he says. "Keep it up! There is a SIG helicopter waiting for you at Logan Airport. It will take you to the *Arcturus,* a schooner we have chartered to monitor the whales and the Russians. There is a Russian defector on the ship who says he is willing to work for us."

Turn to page 29.

You give the bald man your explanation, keeping a straight face, wondering if you could pass a lie-detector test.

"Tsk, tsk," the bald man says. "I'm very disappointed in you. It's true that we haven't decoded the whalesong, but we have learned something about it. We've learned that it is just the opposite of a warning, for the first part of it is *come* or *follow*. So, Jonah, there is, you must know, only one consequence of lying to us . . ."

As he levels his automatic at you, you realize this is . . .

The End

You fire and miss—twice.

A man in the raft returns your fire. He can hardly hope to aim his automatic KV3 rifle from a raft bobbing up and down in the waves, but he makes a very lucky shot.

The End

You stand up on the bow and raise your hands. Two men are now on deck, pointing their automatic weapons at you.

"Jump in the water," one of them calls, "or we'll blow you in."

You jump. The enemy agents in your boat take the controls, bring it alongside the sub, and climb aboard. A moment later, the sub riddles your boat below the waterline with 20-mm machine-gun fire. It's sinking fast.

You swim clear and tread water, thinking the sub will pick you up. You gauge the distance to the reef. You turn and face the sub. It is coming directly toward you. It's almost upon you—traveling at full speed!

The End

You run along through the dunes, keeping as low as possible. A bullet whistles by your ear, then another. Now you are out of range, running to the dock.

Your SIG training has taught you how to start the engine of any car or boat without a key within thirty seconds. You reach the boat, uncleat the lines, cast them off, and jump aboard.

The tidal current carries the boat away from the dock. You hear footsteps of someone running. You shine your flashlight on the controls, find the ignition, and cut away a plastic panel. A moment later, you have the engine started, and you are accelerating, setting a course to intercept the raft. You hear gunfire, and you keep your head down. You'll be out of range in a moment.

In a few minutes you see the raft up ahead. The KGB agents open fire. You gun the engine and run the boat at high speed toward the raft. At the last moment you veer off and throw the engine into full reverse, setting up waves that overturn the raft.

You bring your boat alongside and let the survivors up one by one, stripping them of their weapons as they come aboard. One of them hauls up a waterproof case, which you hope contains the whalesong tape. You make them lie face down on the dock and head your boat out to sea. Your plan is to round Galey Point and put in at the naval base in Boston—about a sixty-mile trip.

You have a rough time trying to steer, consult your chart, and watch your prisoners at the same time, while your boat pitches and rolls in the lumpy sea.

Suddenly, the waves break in front of you. Something is rising out of the water ahead of

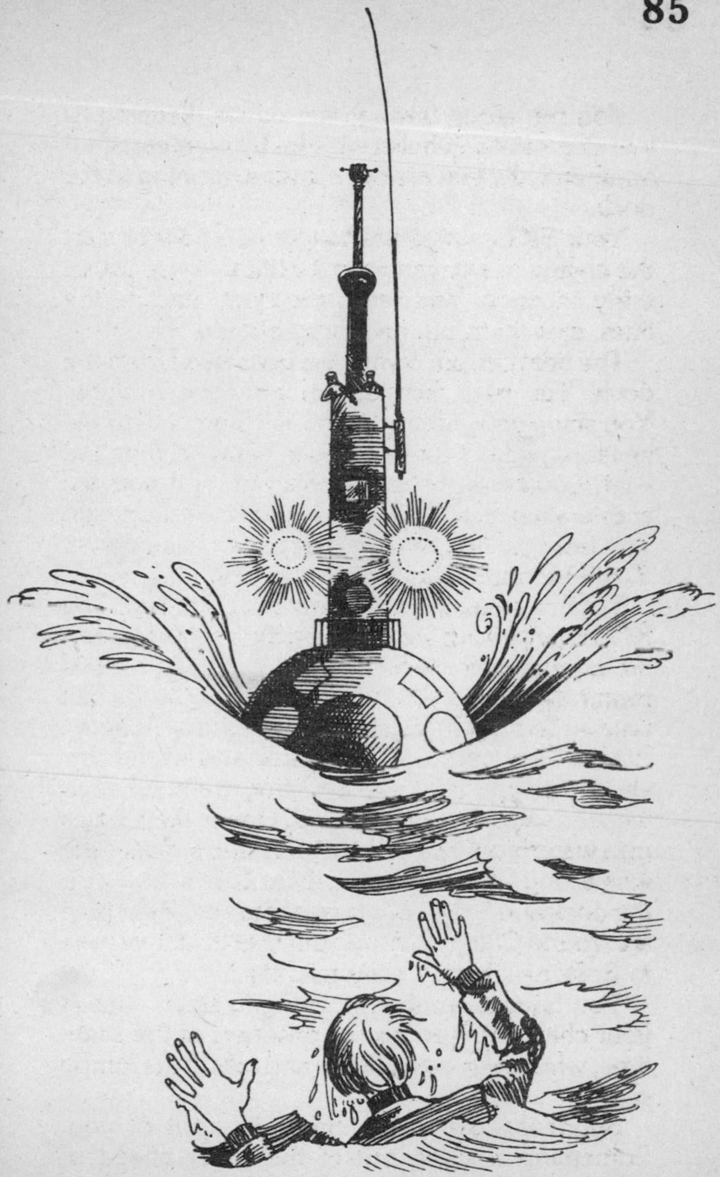

you—a submarine! You reverse engines. The 20-mm gun mounted on the sub rotates until it is pointed directly at you.

"Get up in the bow or we will blow you out of the water!" a voice calls in halting English.

If you follow the instructions, turn to page 83.

If you pursue the only possible escape route by diving into the cabin and then running your boat directly toward the shore, turn to page 87.

You veer off toward the shore and throw the throttle on full. You crouch low, keeping your head only high enough to see where you're going, as a hail of heavy-caliber bullets rips into the boat. The water is getting shallow. The sub can no longer follow, and the range is increasing. By a miracle you haven't been hit, but the engine is on fire. The enemy agents are nowhere to be seen. They must have jumped overboard.

Now the whole stern is in flames. You run forward and dive off the bow. You swim underwater as fast as you can. Then you hear a muffled sound and feel the shock wave of an explosion.

As you surface, you see that the whole stern of the boat must have been blown off, for there is nothing visible but the fast-disappearing bow.

You start swimming for shore. It's still quite a distance, but the sea is fairly calm. You think you can make it, as long as you don't panic. Anxiously you glance around. There is something bobbing in the water a little further out from shore than you are. It looks like a small rubber raft that must have been blown clear in the explosion. It's clearly within swimming distance, yet, once you reach it, the wind and current may carry you out to sea.

*If you try to make it to the beach,
turn to page 107.*

*If you swim for the raft,
turn to page 108.*

As soon as you tell of your conversation with Mrs. DuMont, Obbard orders you to return to Washington. A few hours later, you are once again seated at the big oak desk, while Obbard stares at you, holding a pack of matches in one hand and his pipe in the other—apparently too preoccupied to light it.

"A huge, protected cavern in the Arctic, twenty kilometers across—a whole country, owned and occupied by whales, talking whales." Obbard tilts back in his chair and gazes up at the ceiling dramatically as he summarizes your report. "You'll have to tell the president about this! You know what he'll do, don't you? He'll want to send a submarine expedition in there."

"Yes," you reply, "he won't wait for any invitation from the whales."

You feel torn between your chosen career as a spy and your distaste for the human invasion of the cavern of the whales.

If you go with Obbard to brief the president, turn to page 90.

If you decide to resign and undertake a new career as a marine biologist, turn to page 93.

"I just don't feel I'm getting anywhere," you tell Obbard.

"Don't worry about it," Obbard replies. "I have a plane waiting to take you to the *Arcturus*, a diesel schooner we have chartered to monitor Russian experiments with the whales. The skipper reports they have a Russian spy on the ship who has defected and is willing to turn over valuable information."

Turn to page 29.

"Usually I have to wait two or three days to see the president, but when he heard that we have a major break on the whalesong, he wanted us to come right over," Obbard says, while the two of you are waiting outside the Oval Office.

A few minutes later the door opens, and an aide ushers you in and introduces you to the president.

"So you've come up with something big," the president says, as he shakes your hand.

Obbard gestures to you, and once again you recount your conversation with Mrs. DuMont.

The president thinks a long time before he replies.

"It is in the interests of the United States," he finally says, "to prevent military competition for the cavern of the whales. I shall purpose a treaty reserving it solely for these great and gentle creatures."

You feel happy that, at least for the present, the welfare of the whales is in the interests of the United States.

The End

"I'm working for the Special Intelligence Group, not for anyone else," you say.

"I'm sure they will always remember you as a hero," one of the thugs says, as he pulls the trigger.

The End

Obbard is surprised at your unexpected decision.

"You can't resign!" he replies. "We can't afford to lose a top agent like you. It's not done. It's unpatriotic. Look, I'll see that you get a good raise."

"No, money is not the issue," you reply, "nor patriotism, for that matter. Because I know that I can do the most for my country by doing the kind of work that really appeals to me. I want to learn about whales, instead of exploiting them—so I am going to study marine biology."

"I wish you good luck," Obbard says. "But don't get the idea that being a spy is immoral. After all, we are the eyes of freedom!"

He gets up from his chair to emphasize his point.

"Maybe," you think aloud, as you shake hands good-by. A few minutes later you walk out into the bright sunshine—glad to be starting a new life.

The End

You nod and pick up the phone. The caller identifies himself as Claude DuMont. He tells you he is being held at a house on Cape Cod, Massachusetts.

"The only way you can save the whales is to get Russian cooperation," you say. "U.S. submarines are already destroying the whales so the Russians can't learn their secrets. If they learn that the Russians already know, they will stop."

"I understand," DuMont says.

You hope he understands you were lying.

One of the thugs grabs the phone and talks into it. The other one looks at you quizzically, then says, "You did okay. I'll chain you to your bed. We may need your services again."

He marches you down the hall.

"Hey, Vladimir," the other one calls.

At that moment, you see a chance to break away. You run into a bathroom, lock the door, climb out the window, and jump, just in time to escape a hail of bullets. You land with a thud on the mushy ground, pick yourself up, and run.

Go on to the next page.

Half an hour later, you are on the phone with Obbard.

"Very good," he says. "Get a plane to Provincetown. Charter it if you have to. Special agents will meet you. We'll close in on their headquarters by sundown."

Eighty minutes later, when you step off the plane, Agent L-3 is waiting to meet you.

"The mission is ended," she says. "DuMont has been released. The Russian spies have been picked up by one of their subs. They think DuMont told them everything—but he didn't. You see—that wasn't DuMont you talked to, it was Anton Roudnitska. He's been working for us!"

The End

You shoot the rope up to the attic window. The grapple hooks onto the windowsill. You pull yourself up the side of the house, hand over hand. Once inside, you cautiously descend the attic steps to a door and push it slightly open. You can hear voices from downstairs.

You set up your eavesdropping equipment. In a moment you can hear every word of the conversation below:

First voice: "Yes, I just talked to them. They say DuMont wouldn't talk. They've pretty much given up trying to get anything out of him."

Second voice: "Did they feel he knows the secret of the whales?"

First voice: "Yes, but he can't be forced to tell. He has to be tricked into telling; but it won't matter—once we get the tape out to the *Volga*."

Second voice: "Yes, that's . . . when?"

First voice: "At dusk—from Galey Point lighthouse in Provincetown—tonight."

You've heard all you need to. You need to get safely away and intercept that tape. You let yourself down the rope and run into the woods. Three hours later, you are walking through the dunes at Provincetown.

Turn to page 38.

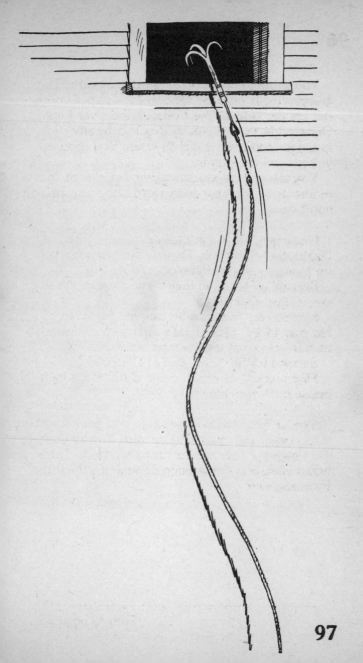

You knock three times before the door slowly opens.

"Yes," answers the chilling voice of a squat, puffy-faced man with slick black hair. "What is it you want?"

"I've been sent to join you by Double-Eye."

"Come in. We need you. I'm Bulkov."

"I'm former U.S. Agent K-3, now working for Double-Eye," you reply.

"Very, very good," Bulkov says. "You'll be glad to see he's here and ready to give you your next order."

He gestures toward another man, who stands holding an 8-mm Luger.

"Your next order," he says, "is to *die*."

The End

"We must meet them," you say.

"Hardalee," the captain calls. "Steer 090."

The sails shake as the bow crosses the wind. A moment later the *Arcturus* heels sharply on the new tack.

"Now we're heading right at them," the captain tells you. "The helmsman is sounding a foghorn now every minute. The Russian sub can hear us if it's on the surface."

"I've lost them on the scanner," a crewman calls up. "They must be almost right on top of us!"

Suddenly, you feel as if you are in the middle of a thundercloud. The *Arcturus* lifts up out of the ocean and heels over sharply. Above the rolling roar you hear the screeching sound of timbers splitting under the strain.

"They're surfacing right under us!" the captain yells. He is clinging to the binnacle, as is the helmsman to the wheel. You crash into the cockpit coaming and clutch wildly at the mainsheet to keep from going overboard.

Go on to the next page.

The *Arcturus* is splitting open.

Water is gushing up. Waves are breaking over the deck.

"Do you think they did it on purpose?" the captain asks.

You shrug your shoulders.

"It looks like we're going down," you say.

"I'm afraid so," the captain replies.

The helmsman is inflating a life raft and preparing to launch it. An enormous wave is coming toward you.

"Launch the raft," the captain shouts. "Jump!"

The three of you jump in the raft and push off as the *Arcturus* flips up its stern and plummets beneath the surface, carrying the rest of the crew and the Russian defector to a watery grave.

The captain says a prayer and then turns toward you.

"I don't think they'll find us in this fog," he says. "Shall I attract them with our electronic beeper? If I don't, I imagine we'll be rescued within a couple of days."

If you say yes, turn to page 103.

If you say no, turn to page 105.

"Let's sail away from here," you say.

Lindstrom immediately orders the helmsman to bear off and head toward the Cape. The *Arcturus* moves gently through the waves. The booms swing out. With the wind on the quarter now, it gathers speed, cutting gently and silently through the sea.

"We won't sound the foghorn," the captain says. "There is hardly much danger of collision. We're out of the shipping lanes."

After a few hours' travel, the *Arcturus* picks up a radio message. You decode it. It's from Obbard!

"Operation canceled," it reads. "Accord reached with Russians. Whales to be fully protected. Details on your return."

"I'm glad," you tell Lindstrom, "because now, if I ever meet a whale, I won't be ashamed to look it in the eye."

The End

"Yes, we'd best encounter them," you say.

The captain activates the beeper. Within a few minutes the Russian sub comes alongside and brings you aboard. Soon you are warming yourself, drinking Russian soup in the wardroom.

The commander of the sub speaks to you in halting English. "First of all, I am sorry we sank your boat," he says. "It was a beautiful boat. Of course we did not want to sink it. It was an accident. Now all we can do is offer you good soup."

He laughs a bit, and you smile back—relieved at his courtesy, but not ready to trust him.

Turn to page 104.

"You will be glad to know," he continues, "we have learned the secret of the whales, even as we were trying to get your Dr. DuMont to give this information himself. Our first thought was to use the cavern of the whales as a military base, but we decided against it—because one H-bomb would seal the cavern forever. That is why, only half an hour ago, our premier and your president reached an agreement over the hot line: the cavern will be preserved for the whales forever. And, you will be glad to know, we have made arrangements to transfer you to an American submarine in about an hour."

"So the whales will be saved, not through good sense of human beings, but only through good luck," Captain Lindstrom observes.

"Yes, the whales needed good luck to survive, and the same may be said for mankind," the Russian captain says.

The next day you are picked up from the Russian sub by helicopter and returned to Provincetown, where a message from Obbard awaits you saying you've earned a two-week vacation!

Soon you are lying on the sandy beach, soaking up the sun. After a while, you might try surfing, but you've been underwater enough lately. It's nice just feeling the warm sun and sifting sand through your fingers, while you lie gazing up at the puffy white clouds drifting across the sky.

The End

You sit with the others, waiting, rocking, queasy from the motion of the sea, slightly afraid. But you are relieved at having, for the first time in a long time, the chance simply to rest and look up at the sky and think, knowing there will be no ringing of the phone, no knocking on the door.

Your peace and quiet end a few hours later when a U.S. Navy helicopter swoops down to rescue you. With it comes a message from Obbard, ordering you to Provincetown Hospital to visit Don Taylor, a British Intelligence agent, who was attacked by KGB agents while he was investigating their activities in the whalesong project.

Turn to page 18

"It surprises me, but I believe you are telling the truth," the bald man says. "You see, we decoded the first part of the whalesong. We knew it meant *come* or *follow,* and you have confirmed that. But follow *where?* —to *what* secret place?"

"I don't know" you reply, as you reach for the $10,000.

"Not so fast," the bald man says. "You've earned some of that, but not all. You'll get $5,000 now and $5,000 when you find out for us what the rest of the message is—*where do the whales go?* That's what we want. Will you do it?"

You nod affirmatively.

"Do not betray us, or we shall spare no expense to liquidate you."

Two guards usher you out onto the street. You return to your hotel and call Obbard to report on what happened.

"Good work!" he says. "On the basis of the information you've obtained, we can get a warrant to go in and recover the whalesong tape and break up the biggest spy operation in the country."

"Thanks," you say.

You feel good about what you have accomplished. Life should be good for a while, but you wonder how long you will be around to enjoy it.

The End

You swim slowly but steadily, pacing yourself to conserve your strength. You pause for a moment to gauge your distance to the shore. You are almost halfway there, but the current has carried you down the beach toward a point of land jutting into the sea. If you keep swimming straight toward the beach the tide may carry you past the point and out to sea before you can touch bottom. What's the best direction in which to swim?

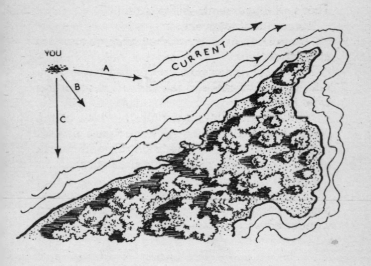

If you swim course A, turn to page 110.

If you swim course B, turn to page 111.

If you swim course C, turn to page 112.

It takes you only a few minutes to reach the raft, but, just as you are about to grab hold, a puff of wind blows it out of reach. You swim as fast as you can, but you are tiring rapidly. Finally with your last ounce of strength you reach up and grasp the rubber rim. With a tremendous effort you heave yourself aboard, and sit shivering in the freshening breeze.

Instantly you realize that all chance of getting ashore is gone. The new wind is blowing off the shore and will rapidly take you out to sea. Your chance of being rescued before daybreak is slim indeed. And if the wind continues to increase, your raft may capsize in the mounting seas. You curl up and lie still, trying to conserve as much strength and warmth as possible.

Resting your head against the rim of your raft, you doze off to sleep. It seems only a moment has passed when you are awakened by the strange and beautiful sounds of the humpback whales. Startled, you sit bolt upright, almost upsetting your raft. In the fading orange glow of twilight you can see them all around you. How many you cannot tell because some are hidden below the surface while others are rolling over and over, making waves that dangerously rock your raft. Two of the whales lie on the surface and wave their huge white flippers in the air. They seem to be waving at you! Another one breaches the waves and raises its fifty-foot-long body almost entirely out of the water before flopping over with a thunderous splash.

You are so awed by the display that you fail to notice the tall two-masted sailing ship—a trim schooner under full sail—bearing down on you, until you hear its sheets running and canvas flapping in the wind as it turns sharply and coasts toward you.

"We're coming alongside!" a voice shouts.

Suddenly the whales have sounded, and you watch with amazement as the schooner eases gently alongside your raft and a crewman lowers a line with a life ring. As soon as you get a grip on it, they haul you aboard.

"Thanks a million for finding me," you tell the captain a moment later.

"The whales found you for us," he replies modestly.

"Then I'll thank them too," you reply, and you resolve to find a way to do that—even if it means giving up your career as a spy!

The End

You swim diagonally away from the point of land, pulling steadily, arm over water, breathing, kicking, yet trying to save your strength.

You're making headway against the current; it hasn't swept you any closer to the point. But you notice that you are still almost as far from the beach as you were before. You feel your strength ebbing; yet you swim on. Finally, exhausted, you realize you have given your all. You just aren't going to make it.

The End

You swim as hard as you can, directly toward the beach. You make good progress, but the current is sweeping you faster and faster toward the point. If you can't touch bottom before you pass the point, you won't stand a chance. Now your arms feel like lead weights. Numb with cold, you struggle on a few moments, then feel yourself slipping beneath the waves. . . .

Hoowoop, hoowoop, hoowoop—eerie and beautiful sounds reach your ears, bringing you to life. Dimly you realize you are hearing the song of a humpback whale! In a moment other whales join in—singing the new whalesong. At the same time you feel a surge of energy throughout your body, coupled with an overwhelming urge to live!

You start swimming again—faster. In a few moments you are close to the point; the current is sweeping you past it; you try to touch, and, for a second, feel the sand brushing against your toes. You stroke furiously. Suddenly you are standing! Still fighting the current, you wade ashore and drop exhausted on the sand.

A moment later, looking out over the misty sea, you see a spout of water, then another further away. You hold your hand up in salute. Do the whales know that their song gave you the strength to make it to shore? Somehow you feel sure of it.

The End

You strike out toward the point, and you seem to be swimming faster than ever, as you rapidly approach your destination. Then you realize that, though you are much closer to the point, you are already opposite it, and the current is carrying you away from it. You swim a few strokes against the tide, but it is hopeless. There is nothing to do but stay afloat as long as you can and hope a boat will pick you up. *Then there is no hope—a gigantic gray shark is heading right at you!*

But it is not a shark! The great gray shape before you is the head of a humpback whale, and suddenly it has scooped you up with its wedge-shaped snout. The whale is propelling you through the water at terrific speed. You gasp for air and think of a prayer as you fly through waterfalls of foam and spray. Then with a violent wrench you are flipped into calm water; the whale has turned its great body and is swimming out to sea.

You look around and see that you are far down the beach, only a few dozen yards from shore! A moment later you pull yourself up and lie exhausted in the sand, forever a friend of the humpback whale.

The End

You tell McKim you'll have to think it over and let your conscience be your guide. You shake hands and bid him good day. A few hours later, when you get a phone call from Obbard, you still haven't made up your mind. To your surprise, Obbard already knows about your conversation with McKim.

"You're fired," he tells you. "We have a saying in the Special Intelligence Group: if you have to let your conscience be your guide, you'll never make it as a spy."

The End

ABOUT THE AUTHOR

A graduate of Princeton University and Columbia Law School, EDWARD PACKARD lives in New York City, where he is a practicing lawyer. Mr. Packard conceived of the idea for the Choose Your Own Adventure® series in the course of telling bedtime stories to his children, Caroline, Andrea, and Wells.

ABOUT THE ILLUSTRATOR

PAUL GRANGER is a prize-winning illustrator and painter.

CHOOSE YOUR OWN ADVENTURE®

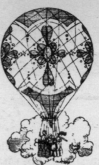

You'll want all the books in the exciting *Choose Your Own Adventure*® series offering you hundreds of fantasy adventures without ever leaving your chair. Each book takes you through an adventure—under the sea, in a space colony, on a volcanic island—in which you become the main character. What happens next in the story depends on the choices *you* make and *only you* can decide how the story ends!

Rancho Rosal School
3535 Village at the Park Drive
Camarillo, CA 93012